Let's Share and Get Along

Charlene Noble

To order additional copies of this book, contact:
Xlibris
844-714-8691
www.Xlibris.com
Orders@Xlibris.com

ISBN: 978-1-6641-4579-5 (sc)
ISBN: 978-1-6641-4578-8 (hc)
ISBN: 978-1-6641-4580-1 (e)

Print information available on the last page

Rev. date: 08/18/2022

Let's Share and Get Along

By
Charlene Noble

LET'S SHARE AND GET ALONG

Sprawled on the flowery living room rug, toys scattered around her, Sparka observantly counted her toys.

"One, two, three, four," she counted as she handled each one and continued to reach in a big brown bag for a few Johnni Swells. She licked her red lips, enjoying the cherry taste of the candy.

As Sparka caressed her dolly, and ran the comb slowly through her curly red hair, she was distracted by a loud yelp. She dashed to the window to look.

Oh, it's just Daio playing all by herself, she thought.

Oh, there's Tyra, I didn't see her. It seems as if they're having fun. Wonder should I join them.

Sparka thought heavily as her fingers wrapped tightly around her long, black braid. Her big, brown eyes got tired of watching the girls jumping up and down, and the rope going around and around, so she joined them.

"You missed, it's my turn," exclaimed Sparka as she stopped turning the rope. "Take my end, Daio, here, take it!"

The girls jumped rope continuously until they couldn't jump any longer.

"Let's rest," said Sparka, exhausted. "Let's sit on my front lawn."

"Hey, Sparka, I see your dolly is keeping an eye on you," Tyra said jokingly, as she glanced up at the window.

"I forgot that I left her there," Sparka said. She glanced up and waved at her dolly. "Come on, girls, let's sit down."

Not used to sharing without encouragement, Sparka pulled out a piece of candy, and unwrapped it in front of the girls.

The girls looked at each other in surprise. They looked at Sparka and asked politely in unison, "May we have one?

Sparka was shocked. "I'll be back," she said, rising to go indoors. "I'm going to get dolly."

Sparka was alone again. She had no idea the girls would want something that belonged to her.

Sparka skipped cheerfully into the living room, but suddenly stopped when she saw her little brother running her toy across the floor. She kneeled down beside him and pretended to play along, then slyly eased the truck from his hand.

"Why can't I play with your truck?" Newbie asked angrily.

"It's not yours," she replied loudly. "You have toys, play with them."

That night, Sparka sat on the couch watching television. "Oh, mister blue, blue, blue, I'm ashamed of you, you, you," she sang along with the lady on the television.

Newbie glanced up at her then he went on rolling this truck playfully across the floor. Not paying any attention to her brother, Sparka secretly ate her candy.

"Ah,ah, what are you eating?" he asked surprisedly. "Nothing," she said leaping to turn the channel. Sparka jumped up so quickly that a piece of candy dropped from her pocket.

"Nothing, huh!" Newbie replied angrily. "I saw your mouth moving up and down. Why don't you ever share?"

"What are you saying?" Sparka asked. "I was filling my mouth with air and blowing it out."

"Look, I have the candy in my hand," Newbie said, holding it out.

When Saprka saw the candy in her brother's hand, she rushed toward him to wrestle for it. They rolled on the floor.

"Let me have it," she exclaimed as she sat on top of him trying to pull the candy from his closed hand.

"No" yelled Newbie as he tried to push her off him. "It's mine, I found it." He clenched his fingers tightly. The more Sparka tried to pull his fingers apart, he clinched tighter. Suddenly, Newbie pushed her off him then tossed the candy to her.

"There, you can have it," he said panting. 'I guess you forgot about the Bible verse Grandma reads that says, "Give to those that ask, and never turn your back on those who borrow.' Remember, Mom says we have to get along.

Sparka was happy to get her candy back and pretended not to hear Newbie as she continued to watch television.

The following morning, Sparka was awakened by bright sunlight, and by the sound of horns. She stumbled out of bed to the window.

"A party," she mumbled as she wiped the sleep from her eyes. "What are all those blue, red and orange balloons doing tied to fence and goodies spread over the table. Someone is having a party and didn't tell me."

"It's Newbie's party," she thought. "I didn't know that a seven year old could throw a party like this.

No wonder he didn't tell me about it; he knew I was invited anyway.

Sparka unhesitantly skipped to join them.

"Who invited you?" asked Newbie hostilely.

"I am invited, aren't I?" Sparka asked sincerely as she reached for the cookie bag. "Aren't I young enough, recall I'm only nine years old."

"Shhhh," Newbie whispered to the other boys, "She'll leave us alone if we don't talk back." He grabbed the goodies to his side of the table.

Sparka slowly stepped away from the table and sadly strolled into the house. She was hurt. Why was Newbie behaving so selfishly?

Later that evening, Sparka invited her brother to join her at play.

"Newbie, Newbie, come play with me," she called.

She spread her toys about the living room floor as she waited for him.

"Newbie," she called again. "Come here, I have something for you."

"Did you call me?" he asked, as he rushed in the room. His eyes wandered excitedly over the toys. He always got excited over the toys.

"Wow, wee," he yelled as he dropped his truck to play with hers. "Wait, I have something for you, too." He stacked his cookies, pretzels and grapes on the wide silver platter.

"I don't see Daio and Tyra," Sparka said, looking out the window. "I want to invite them, too." When she saw the platter of goodies, a slight smile appeared on her little round face.

"There're Daio and Tyra," said Newbie excitedly as he glanced out the window. "Come on up, girls. We're having an apology party."

"An apology party," Sparka said. "It's just a plain 'ole party. "Come on in girls," she said as they entered the door happily.

"Have a seat," Sparka said. "I apologize for behaving selfishly toward you all. I remember Matthew 5:24. It says, 'Reconcile to thy brother, and then offer thy gift.'

"That's beautiful," said Tyra and Daio simultaneously. "That's the verse Mother often reads to us," Newbie said, "You didn't forget it after all."

"You're right, "Sparka replied." I'll also keep Matthew 5:42 in mind. Listen, let's get started. We will get along from now on."

Printed in the United States
by Baker & Taylor Publisher Services